Rod

Rodcampbell

MEET ALL THESE FRIENDS IN BUZZ BOOKS:

Thomas the Tank Engine
The Animals of Farthing Wood
James Bond Junior
Fireman Sam
Joshua Jones
Rupert
Babar

First published in Great Britain in 1994
by Buzz Books
an imprint of Reed Children's Books
Michelin House, 81 Fulham Road, London SW3 6RB
and Auckland, Melbourne, Singapore and Toronto

ISBN 1 85591 370 4

Printed in Italy by Olivotto

TEST OF FRIENDSHIP

Story by Norman Redfern
Illustrations by Arkadia

Lawrence Limburger was furious. Every time he came up with a brilliant plan, the Biker Mice From Mars messed it up.

"We need to make them fight amongst themselves," he told Karbunkle.

"Split them up, and then get them…one by one!"

Karbunkle nodded.

"You should use a Hostility Ray," he said. "I know just the villain for the job. I'll use the Transport Chamber to bring in the ultimate master of disaster – Evil Eye Weevil!"

The city baseball stadium was deserted, but it was far from quiet. Down on the turf, a fast and furious game was in full swing. There were four players, one ball – and four motorcycles. The Biker Mice were playing football!

The radio blasted out loud rock music. Charley sped across the pitch and passed the ball to Throttle. Vinnie and Modo moved in to intercept. Suddenly, the music faded.

"Newsflash!" said the DJ. "Lawrence Limburger is to clear the Limburger Wildlife Preserve. Looks like it's wipeout time for our furry friends!"

The four bikers skidded to a halt. They were horrified.

"No one hurts *our* furry friends," said Modo. "Let's hit the highway, bro's!"

Three engines roared. One engine stuttered.

"Uh-oh," said Charley. "Bent crankshaft. I'd better head back to the garage. Save that forest, boys!"

Through his powerful binoculars, Lawrence Limburger watched the Biker Mice roar away into the woods.

"Good," he chuckled. "The rats are headed right for my trap!"

Throttle led the way into the wildlife reserve. He looked around. There was no sign of Limburger's felling crew. He skidded to a halt, and Modo and Vinnie joined him.

"Something's wrong, bro's," he murmured.

"Like what?" asked Vinnie.

"Like a trap," replied Throttle.

He was right. Evil Eye Weevil and his friends were waiting in a nearby clearing. They had built a jump ramp for his stunt bike.

Evil soared up the ramp and high over the forest. His evil eye was ready to fire its Hostility Ray. Whoever it hit would become mean and nasty. He aimed at the Biker Mice – and fired!

"Somethin' ugly just flew by," said Throttle.

"What, like your face?" snarled Modo.

"Nah," sneered Vinnie, "like your mother's!"

From the road came the roar of another bike. Charley raced into the clearing to find the Biker Mice, fists clenched, shouting at each other.

"Hey, guys, what's going on?" she asked.

"Shut up, Charley!" they shouted back.

Charley was amazed. The three friends were fighting like enemies. Then Vinnie rode off alone.

"Good riddance," yelled Throttle.

"Yeah? Well, from now on you're on your own," Modo bellowed back.

And he and Throttle took off in opposite directions.

"Something is very wrong here," Charley said to herself.

Suddenly, Evil's friends, Heevee and Hurley, came speeding through the forest.

"Head for the Limburger Tower," Hurley shouted to Heevee.

"I should have guessed," said Charley. "When something stinks, you can bet Limburger's at the bottom of it!"

For once, Limburger was smiling.

"Excellent work," he told Evil and his friends. "Each of the Mice is alone now. But you three are not. Bring me those Biker Mice – or I'll send you all home on tricycles!"

They found Modo at a farm outside the city. The Hostility Ray had worn off. Now he just felt sad.

"I don't know what happened, but I'm not gonna lose my best friends," he said to himself. "I'm gonna find them and make up with them right now."

"Well, isn't that sweet?" chuckled Evil Eye Weevil.

Then Heevee and Hurley closed in and took Modo away.

Vinnie was roaring down the highway when a truck pulled in front of him. He jumped his bike into the air and skidded to a halt on top of the truck.

"I'm Vinnie the Awesome!" he cried. "Who needs Throttle and Modo, anyway?"

Evil Eye Weevil leaned out of the cab. "Right now," he said, "I'd say *you* do!"

Throttle searched everywhere for Vinnie and Modo. It was dark when he returned to the Last Chance Garage. There was no one there, either. Then a bike roared up.

"Throttle!" cried Charley. "I've been looking for you. Limburger's brought in a new villain called Evil Eye – "

"Weevil!" cried Throttle. "He's got a Hostility Ray. That would explain a lot."

Throttle climbed on to his bike.

"Hold the fort, Charley," he said. "I've got to get my biker buddies back!"

Evil Eye Weevil sat in Limburger's office and stared into his pocket mirror.

"Just perfect," he sighed.

Across the room, Vinnie and Modo were held tightly by metal clamps. Limburger gloated as they struggled in vain.

"Two vexatious vermin down, one to go," he sneered.

"One's all it takes," said Vinnie.

"Especially if it's Throttle," said Modo.

"Silence, you raving rodents!" snarled Limburger.

"But, Mr Limburger," began Greasepit. "Look over there!"

Outside, it was dark, but the moon was full. On the roof of the building opposite stood a lone biker. His engine roared and a fiery glow filled the night sky as Throttle soared over the edge of the building.

He smashed through the window of Limburger's office and snatched Evil's mirror from out of his hand. One burst from his ray-blaster cut through the shackles. Vinnie and Modo were free!

"That's our bro'!" cried Modo.

"Don't just sit there – get them!" shouted Limburger.

As Vinnie and Modo leapt for their bikes, Evil Eye Weevil fired his Hostility Ray across the room. But Throttle held the mirror in the path of the ray. The beam bounced off the mirror and covered the Plutarkians in its evil red glow.

Suddenly, Limburger, Greasepit, Evil Eye and his cronies were feeling very mean towards each other. And the meaner Evil Eye felt, the more he blasted his ray around.

"Things could turn ugly, bro's," said Throttle.

"You mean uglier!" said Vinnie. "Let's rock – and ride!"

With a screech of tyres, they raced towards the windows and smashed their way out. The Biker Mice sailed through the air and landed on the ground below. Charley was waiting to greet them.

From Limburger's office came angry shouts, crashes, thumps and bangs.

"Music to my ears," laughed Vinnie.

"Hey," said Throttle, checking his watch. "We can still catch the Chicago Nubs game."

"All right!" grinned Modo. "They're my favourite team!"

"I can think of one I like better," said Charley.

"Like who?" asked Modo.

"Like the Biker Mice From Mars," said Charley.

BIKER
MICE™
FROM
MARS